LOCKED OUT

RAISING HEAVEN

LOCKED OUT

PATRICK JONES

MINNEAPOLIS

Darby Creek
A division of Lerner Publishing Group, Inc.
241 First Avenue North
Minneapolis, MN 55401 USA

For reading levels and more information, look up this title at
www.lernerbooks.com.

The images in this book are used with the permission of: © Creatista/iStock/
Thinkstock (young woman); © iStockphoto.com/DaydreamsGirl (stone); ©
Maxriesgo/Dreamstime.com (prison wall) © Clearviewstock/Dreamstime.com,
(prison cell).

Main body text set in Janson Text LT Std 12/17.5.
Typeface provided by Adobe Systems.

Library of Congress Cataloging-in-Publication Data

Jones, Patrick, 1961–
       Raising Heaven / by Patrick Jones.
          pages   cm. — (Locked out)
       Summary: Seventeen years after she was born to a prison inmate, Deja
    agrees to raise her newest half-sister for the first six months, until their
    mother's next release, but despite the help of friends and relatives and a
    support program at school, caring for a baby proves to be a monumental
    task.
       ISBN 978–1–4677–5802–4 (lib. bdg. : alk. paper)
       ISBN 978–1–4677–6186–4 (eBook)
       [1. Prisoners' families—Fiction. 2. Mothers and daughters—Fiction.
    3. Babies—Fiction. 4. African Americans—Fiction. 5. Houston (Tex.)—
    Fiction.] I. Title.
    PZ7.J7242Rai 2015
    [Fic]—dc23   2014018198

Manufactured in the United States of America
1 – SB – 12/31/14

To the Isis Rising Prison Doula Project of
Everyday Miracles
—P.J.

1

I was born in prison.

Well, that's not honest. They released Mom for the day, took her to a county hospital in cuffs, and with two guards watching, the docs cut me out of her. That was seventeen years ago.

Now, she's back inside, this time in the county workhouse doing a year straight time for violating her parole—again—and drug charges—again—and she's pregnant—again. She's been pregnant a bunch of times between me and my half-sister who'll be born in a few months. Some she got rid of, a couple she had, but most never made it. The county took me from her soon after I was born, but Grams got custody, unlike my half-sibs who came later. They're in foster care or adopted, but still among the millions of people in Houston. I don't see much of 'em and that's OK with me. We got different dads, and I don't really feel attached to them.

But the one on the way—she's different. I'm gonna help raise this one. Since Mom's only doing a year, it's not enough time to lose her parental rights. She'll have the baby at the county hospital, they'll bring it home to Grams, and we'll take care of her until Mom's home in six months.

And this time Mom says she's getting clean and staying clean. This time she says she's going to be a good mom. This time she says everything's going to be different.

Nothing we ain't heard before. I think that's what breaks Grams's back: not raising me, not taking Mom in when she's out, not working hard for hardly any money. What breaks Grams is Mom breaking her promises. If Mom would say, "I'm an addict, I'm gonna use," then she'd accept that: that's who you are. We don't like it, but we get it. Instead, every time Mom comes out, it's all about "getting clean" and "starting over" and "working the program." But they're all just words.

Used to be every time Mom broke a promise, it broke my heart a little bit more. But now I got no trust left to shatter, no hopes to be crushed. That's for little kids, and I ain't been one of those for a long time. Mom stole my childhood along with all the money, drugs, cars, and jewelry she took.

I can't get that back, but I can get the next best thing. I can make sure this baby's life don't turn out like mine. I'll raise up a sweet child the right way, and unlike Mom, I won't break my promises.

2

My cousin Malik, who came here after Katrina, has this bit about Houston whenever he meets somebody who's just moved here. He says, "I know I'm going to Heaven 'cos I spend my time in Hell." Then he asks the person, "You know the difference between Hell and Houston?" And the person says "I don't know" and then Malik says, "Hell's got less people and a better climate!" Most people laugh. Until they've been here awhile. Then it ain't funny, especially in summer, like now.

Me and Malik are walking home together after school—late, 'cos he had an Honor Society meeting. While I was waiting for him, I looked up baby names online. I keep a list of names on my phone. Whenever I find a name I like, it goes on the list. Now, I run a few of 'em by Malik while we walk.

"That's nice," he says every time I read one off for him. He knows Mom's letting me pick the name for her new baby 'cos I'm gonna be taking care of her. Malik is gonna help out too, but he don't get a vote on the name.

It's a long walk home. We live in the Fifth Ward. You know you're getting close when you start to hear sirens.

We're used to walking, even in this heat. Hardly anybody in the Fifth has a car. Aunt Beatrice, Malik's mom, drives a beater about as old as me that only starts half the time. I got my license, but I don't drive. I ain't got nowhere to go 'cept school—Malik, my friends like Shanice, and Grams are all in the Fifth. My "Big Sister," Molly, takes me to the downtown library sometimes, but I feel like a space alien there.

One time when me and Malik was walking back from school late like today, he said, "Deja, let's count the men we see on the way home." I don't think we saw a dozen. "It's like a vacuum cleaner sucked up 'em up," Malik said. Except we know the vacuum is the workhouse like my mom's at, the state prison like his dad's at, or the cemetery.

Most men you do see are running the corners. Something about those corners: they draw people to 'em like magnets, thinking they'll find gold, but mostly they find lead. That's what happened to Derek, my daddy. He ain't the only one.

Malik says he's not gonna be like that. He says I ain't gonna be like that neither. We made a promise to each other in junior high that we weren't doing time. We was gonna stay out of trouble, not do drugs, stay in school, graduate, all that. So far, so good.

"You got the baby's room ready?" Malik asks. He says it all playful, 'cos the baby's room is really just my room.

"Almost," I say. "I found my old crib boxed up in the storage room." The storage room is Mom's room. She don't use it much even when she ain't locked up, so Grams keeps all kinds of junk in there.

I don't mention what else I found in that room. There was a cardboard box full of letters Derek wrote to Mom when one or the other of them was on the inside. They're all the same— love he didn't provide, promises he didn't keep. She'd write back the same things. When they were together on the outs, they'd try to make it work. They'd get clean while they were locked up, but it never stuck. It takes months to get into a program; it takes minutes to score on the corner.

I ain't mentioned those letters to anybody, not even Grams. Especially not her.

To hear Grams tell it, it wasn't her fault. She raised all her kids right. The fact that "right" means "go right to jail" for two of the three don't faze her none. She says Carla was a good kid till Derek "led her down a dark path."

I don't remember Derek much. Before he got his one-way ticket to the cemetery he was usually locked up, out late, or with another woman. But when he'd come around, Mom would use me like some chip in a poker game. She'd say, "If you want to see Deja, you'll straighten yourself out." Since he never got straight, it means he didn't want to see me, which means he didn't love me. I don't think of Derek as my dad. He was a donor, not an owner.

I think that's why me and Malik is such good friends, and why he says he's gonna be around to help out with the baby. Like he wants to be the dad neither of us ever had.

"You gotta have one of those spinny things," Malik says. "To hang over the crib. A mobile. I'll ask Shanice if she knows where we can get one."

I just laugh. "I'm more worried about bottles and diapers and onesies than I am about spinny things."

"Nah, we'll get one," Malik insists. I bet Shanice knows all about mobiles. I bet she had all kinds of toys when she was a baby. I love Shanice—she'd be my best friend even if she wasn't Malik's girlfriend—but her folks probably had more money to spend on mobiles than Grams has to spend on groceries.

I don't say that to Malik, though. I just tell him, "You're gonna be the baby's favorite cousin-slash-uncle."

Malik smiles. "This baby's gonna be the future," he says. "She won't grow up with the past we inherited, filled with our parents' mistakes."

That's what I'm hoping. It's the only hope I got.

3

FOUR WEEKS BEFORE DUE DATE

Sunday service at our church is always full. I'm there with Malik, Shanice, and Aunt Beatrice. Even in this heat, we're still dressed up because Beatrice demands it.

Maybe because it's hot as Hell, Pastor Green talks a lot about the kingdom of Heaven. I can't say I'm paying that much attention. I'm only here to keep Aunt Beatrice off my back. She's the good one in the family—the middle child. Mom's the youngest, and Clinton's the oldest. Clinton's doing life in Huntsville.

After the service is over, we catch the bus back to Grams's house where everybody gathers most every Sunday after church. It's a big family—Grams has five sibs, and everybody takes care of each other. The say it takes a village to raise a child. Grams's family is our own village, 'cept year by year the men leave the village and don't come back.

I relax into my seat. The seats of this city bus are a lot nicer than the ones on the prison shuttles I used to take to visit Mom. At least this time when Mom messed up she only got County time, so I spend less time on those buses.

"So Deja, you getting excited?" Shanice asks.

"Yeah, and a little nervous," I admit. I spent the first week after school hunkered down in the Fifth Ward library—which has AC, unlike home—reading books and printing out Internet articles on raising babies. But instead of feeling prepared, now I'm just scared awful. "Wouldn't you be if it was you?"

"Deja, I wouldn't be doing what you're doing," Shanice says. "I mean, I'll support you and help out how I can, but a baby—don't matter if it isn't your own. That's hard work."

"Most things are." For me, that's always been

true. For Shanice, not so much. She's used to having two parents with jobs, a home with AC, teachers fawning over how smart she is, having life come easy to her.

"Besides, Grams is gonna help out," I add.

Aunt Beatrice snorts like a cartoon bull. "You believe that?"

"She told me she'd help out all she could," I say, too loud.

Beatrice shakes her head and offers up this sad little smile. "She didn't help me none," she says. "If I recall, she didn't help your mother that much when you were little either. She acted like she was helping, made a big deal of every little thing she did, but in the end it was only what she felt like doing. She didn't strain herself. She wasn't no superhero and she wasn't no saint."

I can't argue with her because I don't remember much from that time. What I do remember, I wish I could forget. Seems like I cried a lot, holding up my arms for someone to pick me up, but nobody did. Maybe the reason I'm strong like Molly said is 'cos I had to pull myself up alone. It shouldn't be that way. I don't want another kid in my family to go through that. I'll be those loving arms reaching down.

"Your mom was too young to have a baby then," Beatrice says, "And too old to have one now." That's kind of true. Mom's only thirty-two, but she's lived hard more than half those years.

I change the subject. "Hey, Malik, I told Molly your joke about the difference between Hell and Houston. She liked it." He laughs.

"So, if Hell is like Houston," I add, "what do you think Heaven is like?"

Malik starts to answer, mainly by repeating a lot of the stuff that Pastor Green said. I'm listening, but I'm looking out the windows at the Fifth. So many of these stores, houses, and cars empty inside, but outside, full of gang tags.

"I think Heaven is like your own dream and it's different for everybody," Shanice says.

"If that's true, I'm in Heaven right now," says Malik, "'cos I'm living a dream with an angel by my side." My cuz gives me cavities with such sweetness. "What do you think, Deja?" he asks.

I glance at the women and children on the bus. I think about the women and children on the prisons buses over the years, then say, "Heaven is a place where nobody makes any mistakes."

4

"Deja, how do you plan on managing this responsibility?" Molly asks me. "Even if it's only for a few months, it's still a lot of work and worry." We're sitting at this fancy coffee shop way outside the Fifth Ward. Molly's always try-ing to take me places that'll "expand my hori-zons," but usually that just means somewhere with AC that's far away from the Fifth.

Molly's OK. She's the third woman I've had in the Big Sister program since Mom signed me up way-back-when. I'll say this about Mom: she knows how to get stuff. She signs up for every program there is. Well, except rehab. Not 'cos she hasn't wanted to. But there's always a waiting list that's almost as long as her sentence. And Mom's not much good at waiting.

I suck down the most expensive, fattening drink they sell and answer Molly's question. "I got it all planned," I say. "Planning is something I do well. And I got lots of support. My grandma will help, and my cousin Malik, and my friend Shanice."

"That's wonderful." She's drinking some fancy, nasty-smelling tea. "When's the baby due?"

"Beginning of August, a few weeks before school starts."

"Does your school have a program for young mothers?"

"Yeah. They said they'd make an exception and let me in even though it's not my baby."

"Remind me what school you go to?"

"Harriet Jacobs High School."

She types on her tablet. I'd like one of those. Or any computer. Even my school doesn't have many computers. After a hurricane years ago, people looted the school. Even after all this time, the school hasn't replaced all the stolen machines.

I tell Molly a little about school, but she nods her head like she knows everything already. She's probably looking us up online 'cos I can tell she's reading her screen, not listening to my words.

"So anyway, they got child care on site, but you also get to spend time with your baby," I explain. She's still reading, not looking at me. It's rude, but I don't say anything. "And the—"

She cuts me off and starts telling me what's on her screen. "The program is tailored to the needs and interests of each student. It offers flexibility and choice, recognizing the unique gifts and passions of each child, as well as each child's challenges and obstacles to learning. So, Deja, what obstacles do you think you'll face?"

"Well, I don't think I'll know many girls in the program," I confess. "I know 'em 'cos I went to school with them, but they're not friends or anything." Honest, one's my enemy. Yasmin.

"And why is that?" Molly likes asking me questions.

"I ain't like them, being stupid and getting pregnant when they ain't even old enough to drive."

"So you think these girls are stupid for having babies?"

"I think they're stupid for getting pregnant," I say a little too loud. "I mean, the school's got a clinic so it's not like they can't get something. Or maybe they just ought to say no."

Molly laughs at that for some reason but then starts typing again. *Tap tap tap.*

I keep going. "I'm not like model pretty or anything, but I got plenty of boys interested in me. When I tell 'em I'm not interested in *that*, they find somebody who is. Soon word gets around. Everybody knows who gives it up and who don't. I don't."

"You're a confident young woman. That's a quality many women lack, as people, as parents. You sound strong."

"With what I've been through, if I wasn't

strong, I'd be broken in half by now."

"I bet your mom is very proud of you for being so responsible," says Molly, which is the kind of thing people like her say when they run out of advice. She sips her tea. I can tell she's trying to think of what to say next. What to say to a girl with a life she can't even imagine, a life that the Internet can't explain to her.

"How's your mom doing?" she asks after a minute.

"Oh, she's fine." Honest, sometimes I think my mom gets pregnant before she does time because of all the extra attention it gets her. Out here, she's just one more pregnant woman, but inside, she says they treat a pregnant woman special. More food, less work, more time in medical. And more programs too.

"She told me they've got a new program with something called a doula," I say to Molly.

Molly brightens right up. "I've heard of those. *Doula* means 'a woman who serves.' The idea is to give a pregnant woman support . . ."

"Yeah, Mom explained it. She signed up for

it mainly 'cos she's tired of C-sections. Says her belly looks like a road map."

Molly nods. "Having a doula makes you more likely to carry a baby to term and have a natural birth, with the baby on time and at a healthy weight."

Like most of Mom's kids, I was early and underweight. It feels like I've been behind all my life. I'm glad things are gonna be different for this baby.

"Mom says her doula is named Erin and she's really nice," I add.

I bet Erin *is* nice. All these women from these programs—Mollys, Erins, Claires, Ashleys, Kaitlyns, Amys, whatever—are always nice. Big Sisters, doulas, case workers, nutrition counselors, school counselors, after-school tutors, whatever—are always nice.

Molly's back on her tablet. "Found the program! It has a Facebook page." She doesn't say anything for a minute while she reads. Then she starts to nod, like the doula program has her own personal stamp of approval. "This looks great. Sounds like the doula focuses on both the physical and mental health of the expectant mother. There's a lot of positive learning."

I imagine Mom smiling at Erin, and like always, learning nothing.

5

I hate waiting. But that seems to be all I do. Like now. Visiting hours at the workhouse.

There's lots of loud babies in the lobby. I better get used to that sound.

"How long . . . ?" I start to ask Grams. She looks at the wall clock. Count is running late so that puts everything behind.

"Maybe another ten minutes," she answers.

"No, how long you think we've spent waiting for her?" I need Math-Brain Malik to add it up. "Waiting in visiting rooms, standing in line, riding in buses, sitting in court. All of it."

Grams laughs. Not sure why, 'cos it ain't funny. "Too long, but that's OK."

Grams must not mind the wasted time because she's always got a book with her. She makes me bring my schoolwork during the year and books in the summer. I can't be on my phone, nothing except read. At first I hated it, but I'm getting used to it.

"How is it OK?" I demand.

"Well, it's a good lesson." Grams closes her book. "All that waiting gave you time to think about what your mom put this family through. I bet it's half the reason you've never shown any signs of turning out like her. You've seen the consequences."

I don't say anything. She may be right about that. And she's done the right thing dragging me to every jail, workhouse, prison, halfway house, not to mention every trial and sentencing hearing.

"Form a line!" a female correction officer yells. We put our stuff in the locker and join the line. We go through the metal detector, get a pat-down, and hear the rules. At least in County, we get contact.

From a distance, I see Mom, big as a house, at the table right in front. It seems like everybody who comes in says something to her. I recognize a lot of the faces. Like Mom, they've been here over and over again. Some of these women come back so often I think the county must just reserve rooms for 'em.

We do the kiss-and-hug routine, though I can't get my arms around Mom anymore. "How you feeling?" Grams asks her.

It'll be a long time before either Grams or I get a chance to speak again. Mom talks about herself like she's the most interesting person in the world, 'cept all she needs to do is turn her head and she'd know she's not. Other than being pregnant, Mom's just like all these women.

"You picked out a name yet?" Mom asks me finally. When I say no, she starts making suggestions and talking about how the other women in the program are jealous 'cos of what I'm doing.

"I'm sure enough fortunate to have raised such a loving daughter," Mom says.

Grams snorts like Aunt Beatrice did on the bus the other day.

"You saying something about Deja?" snaps Mom.

Grams says nothing, just gets that stiff-upper-lip look. But Mom won't let it go, so finally Grams snaps back, "I'm not saying anything about Deja, but don't act like you raised her. I did."

Mom holds her stomach like the baby's kicking. "Oh, yeah. You're such a great mother. Three kids, two behind bars and the other married to a criminal."

"I did the best I could," Grams says.

"So did I," Mom says. Now they're both looking at me like they want me to decide who's right. What I really think is I raised myself, with some help from Grams. But no way I'm saying that.

"Please," says Grams. "You been getting into trouble since you were little. And it's been one mistake after another ever since . . ."

The guards announce time's up. Mom reaches out, puts her hand on my shoulder and pushes her big self up. "That's why I'm having this baby. When I had Deja, I was a kid. Dewayne, Joseph, Rae, my life was the streets. But this is going to be different."

Grams cuts her off. "You say that every time. *How* is this baby going be different?"

"Just wait and see," says Mom before she turns her back on us and joins the other women on the walk back to their cells.

6

I'm sweating bullets. Me, Malik, and Shanice stand outside Grams's tiny house and sip iced tea in the early August heat. We just finished the last bit of painting in my room—pink to make it ready for the baby girl.

"Thanks for your help," I say. I wonder how many times over the next few months I'll be saying that to Malik, Shanice, and Grams. A lot, I bet.

"Happy to do it," Malik says. Shanice says it too, but she's giving me a worried look.

"I know it's too late and all, but every time I ask about it, you change the subject," Shanice

27

says. I brace myself for what's coming. "How come you doing this for your mom?"

I say nothing because I don't have an answer. Well, I don't have just one answer. There are a hundred little answers, like little streams feeding into a big river.

"I mean, do you think your mom would do the same for you?" Shanice asks. Who made her the quizmaster? "Your senior year, our senior year, it should be fun."

Malik's staying out of it, but he keeps holding her hand. *That's part of it*, I want to say. *Your senior year IS going to be fun 'cos you got a boyfriend, a shot at college, and lots of friends other than me. I got none of that.*

"Folks who don't know will think the baby's yours," she says. "You don't want that." That gets me thinking about Yasmin.

For a while, about a year ago, I did have a boyfriend, Luke, and he was OK about me not giving it up. Or so he said, until Yasmin got in his business. Now she's got his kid and soon I'll have to face her meanness every day.

"It don't matter to me what people think,"

I say. "I told everybody who needs to know I'm doing this for my mom and they're fine with it."

My tone's a slap and Shanice gets this pouty look.

"Sorry, Shanice, I got a lot on my mind." I tell them about the fight between Mom and Grams when we visited County the other day. "Them going at it isn't helping, you know?"

Shanice nods like she understands, but she don't 'cos her life ain't nothing like mine.

"Deja! Let's go," Grams yells from inside. Seems like all Grams does is yell anymore. But she's right, it's time to go. We're headed to the food pantry to look for baby food and other supplies.

Malik and Shanice give me the empty glasses from their iced tea, say good-bye, and walk off all lovey dovey. I head inside to the kitchen, where Grams is waiting. She fishes around in her purse for her keys, and suddenly I notice the deep slump of her shoulders, and the way her whole face sort of sags. There are bags under her eyes and some of her wrinkles are so deep somebody could'a carved 'em with a penknife.

"Grams, you look tired." I walk past her and put the dirty glasses in the sink.

Grams heaves a sigh. "Sometimes, Deja, I feel so young, and the other times, like today, I just don't know."

"You just wait, Mom's baby's gonna make you feel young again." I laugh. She don't.

"You better get a good night's sleep this week," she says. "You won't have too many of those soon."

"I read about what to expect from a newborn." We head back outside into the heat.

"A book can only tell you so much," Grams says. She locks the door and we start toward the bus stop. "Whatever you thought this was going to be like, you're wrong."

I haven't even done anything yet, and she's telling me I done wrong. Maybe Aunt Beatrice was right. Maybe Grams isn't going to help out like she said. Maybe when Mom gets home, she's not going to change and this baby is really going to be my responsibility, not for a few months but for the rest of my life. "I know it's not going to be easy," I tell Grams. "It's going to be hard work. But it'll be worth it."

I think about that baby looking at me with love in her eyes, knowing I won't let anyone harm her. She won't realize, of course, that it's the people in your family who hurt you the most.

7

TWO DAYS BEFORE DUE DATE

I'm trying not to show how nervous I am, especially to Molly. I got my phone in my hand, just waiting for the call that my new sister is here. Mom's not in labor yet, but it's almost time. Which is quite the achievement since Mom always gave birth way early to pipsqueaks like me.

"Don't worry," Molly says as we walk into the downtown library. "The second she goes into labor, you'll get the call."

I wish I could be there with her, but it's not allowed. Mom's still a prisoner, and that means we still have to play by a hundred extra rules.

"What are we doing here now?" I ask Molly.

Of all the places to be and things to do before the baby, it's odd Molly wants to bring me here. But honest, it's 'bout all we have in common. Go figure, a girl growing up in the Fifth Ward doesn't share many interests with a girl from The Woodlands.

"Well, we need to get some books for the baby," Molly answers. She walks real fast toward the children's section. It's pretty quiet, unlike the Fifth Ward branch, which is always filled with people using computers.

"I already checked out lots of books about babies," I remind her. "Plus the stuff you—"

Now she cuts me off. "No, not *about* the baby, but books for you to read *to* the baby."

"Sure enough that's stupid," I say. "Babies don't know no words."

Molly smiles and walks over toward something called board books. "Deja, one of the most important things you can do is read to the baby. Every day, as much as you can. It'll help make your baby smart, ready to learn."

"Seriously?"

Molly goes off talking about brain

development and using words like linguistics and phonic awareness. She says, like always, she'll give me something to read about it. "The more you read to her, the better. It's easy, it's free, and it doesn't hurt."

She takes me over to the board book area and starts talking about different books and what kinds babies like. "My mom never read me no books when I was a baby," I say.

"Isn't that why you're doing this? You wanted to do things different than your mom did?" Molly picks up a book with a smiling baby on the cover. "I know your mom wants to change—"

"Yeah, she says that every time."

"And you're doubtful. I get it. I've heard that from other girls I've sistered who had mothers likes yours." Molly next picks up a book called *Goodnight Moon*. "You're not the only one, and you're not alone in this."

She holds the book out to me. The cover's this peaceful-looking room with a fireplace with a framed picture. Maybe that's what Molly's home looks like, but not ours. I stare at that cover, thinking about what Malik told me months ago. About this baby being the future. A fresh start.

I take the book and hold it in my hands.

8

THE DUE DATE

Mom's in labor. We're at the hospital, just waiting. For once, waiting for something good, not a sentence, a visit, or another disappointment. "I wonder if Mom's shackled to the bed again like she said she was with me," I say.

"I don't know, but I doubt it with Erin in there," Grams says.

"I wish we could see her," I say. "It's not fair that a stranger like Erin gets to be in with her, but we don't."

Grams squeezes my hand so hard it almost hurts. "Your mom thinks of Erin as a friend."

"You think the doula program will help her change?" I ask.

"Some days I don't think anything will help Carla change. She makes the same promises over and over again, to me, to every judge, every probation officer. They put her in prison when she should be in treatment. Then as soon as she gets out, her addiction takes over. Addiction is a prison too."

I think about what it feels like to be hungry, which I've been many times, but I can't imagine what addiction is like, what it would be like for your whole body to be longing for something. "But this time."

"This time, who knows—maybe there's a real chance. The baby's part of it, Erin's part of it, but you're the difference-maker, Deja."

Another squeeze of her hand fills my body with warmth, pride, hope. I got so much emotion running through my veins that I don't know how there's room for blood to move.

"I'm going to do everything right," I say. "I won't make any mistakes."

Grams pats my leg. "Deja, everybody makes mistakes. If you think you won't make any, then you're making it harder on yourself, like your mom does. She has such high hopes when she gets out, but then one thing goes wrong, it all crashes down, and she gives up and starts using."

"I know, but—"

And then the nurse appears, calls Grams's name. "It's a girl. Just over eight pounds."

Grams and I hug each other so tight that our tears get all mixed up.

"The name!" I say, turning back to the nurse. "You need a name for the birth certificate, right?" I pull my phone out the back pocket of my jeans. I still got the list of names on there. But I haven't made a final decision. Now's the time.

"I told Shanice that I'd use her name as the middle name, OK?" I ask Grams.

She nods. "Your mother said it was up to you. You don't need to ask permission."

"We don't need to know right this second," the nurse says. "I do need other information. Could you come with me?" Grams nods and follows. I should choose a name, but all I can think about is what it's going to be like for Mom: holding that baby for two days, and then going back inside. Bringing life into the world, then going back to a place that sucks life out of a person. I dream about finding Mom, picking up the baby, and the three of us running away together.

But that would be a mistake. A mistake that would ruin everything.

And then I know.

"I got the name!" I yell out. Grams and the nurse turn around. "Heaven!"

9

TWO DAYS AFTER THE BIRTH

We're back at the hospital—Grams, Aunt Beatrice, Shanice, Malik, and me—in the emergency waiting room. EMTs rush broken bodies on stretchers into the county hospital. Out one of these doors in about ten minutes, uniformed officers will slowly escort my mom in handcuffs and ankle bracelets back to the workhouse.

"Why aren't we outside the maternity ward?" Shanice asks. I look at Grams, she looks back at me, both of us wondering who's gonna say it.

Shanice is my friend, so I guess it's my job. "They have a special part of the hospital just for prisoners," I say. Mom told me all about it. "It's like a little jail inside the hospital."

"You'd think for something like this, they'd not have to be reminded," Grams says. "Just feel normal doing the most natural thing. But that's not how the county works."

"Erin's in there with Mom," I say.

"What for?" asks Aunt Beatrice. She thinks we should all be asking more for Jesus's help instead of Erin's. "I thought it was just to help her have the baby."

"This is called the separation visit, and Erin's there because it can be a traumatic experience," I say like I'm reading a report in front of the class. Like this is happening to somebody else, not my mom. "She'll visit Mom two more times. Erin also runs a group at the workhouse to help moms stay connected with their kids."

Shanice shakes her head. "One of my aunts got real depressed after her baby was born— I can't imagine what it would be like for your mom, not able to see her baby," she says.

"She's gonna be sad, that's for sure," Beatrice says. "Always is, after she gives up a baby.

Till she starts in on the drugs again."

I ignore that. I'm trying to be nice to Aunt Beatrice since she's giving me a stroller for the baby. She brought it with her today, but I plan to carry Heaven in my arms. I've been practicing with some old dolls I found. There's a whole method to it—you gotta support the head 'cos the baby's neck ain't strong enough on its own yet . . .

"Carla said Erin would take photos," Grams says. "That's part of the doula's job."

"We'll have plenty of photos," Malik says and then starts clicking away with his phone.

Pretty soon everybody's taking pictures, laughing, like it's the best day in the world. And I guess it is, but part of me isn't here in the moment. Part of is me with Mom, wherever she is in this hospital. As Shanice is laughing like she don't have a care in the world, one of the guards —I hope it's a woman—probably just told Mom to put the baby back in the crib. Knowing Mom, she won't do it the first time they ask. I almost imagine them prying Heaven out of Mom's arms. I start to cry.

"Deja, what's wrong?" Grams whispers.

"Nothing."

I wipe my eyes fast. It's stupid, but I don't want to be crying the first time that Heaven sees me.

"She's here," Beatrice says. A nurse hands the baby over to Grams. Shanice and Malik snap so many pictures so fast I think their fingers will go numb.

I'm not tired, but I'm out of breath as I put my arms out in front of me. Grams places Heaven in my arms, and then starts talking to the nurse, while Beatrice starts talking to God.

As I rest all eight pounds of Heaven in my arms, I wish I could just focus on the cute little face below me—huge dark eyes, button nose, the tiniest wisps of black curls. But instead all I can think is how empty my mom's arms will feel tonight in her cell.

10

I can't stop smiling.

And mainly it's because of how much Mom is smiling as she holds Heaven in her arms. "She's a fat little thing," Mom says. Laughs loud and long like I don't remember.

"All she does is eat and sleep," Grams says.

"Sounds like me," Mom chuckles. Grams smiles at Mom, another rare sight. Heaven is doing exactly what I hoped she'd do: bring my family together.

"Eat, sleep, and cry," I say and yawn so big I hear my jaw crack.

"You're rocking her?" Mom gently rocks Heaven in her arms.

"And reading to her," I say.

"What for?" Mom asks. I explain what Molly told me about reading to a baby. Mom laughs again, but it's her "those people are fools" laugh. That's the one I'm used to hearing.

Mom hands Heaven over to Grams and motions for me to come closer to her. I put my chair next to her chair, but she wants me to come closer still. I'm next to her, so close I can smell the nasty cheap detergent they use on the prisoners' clothes. "How you sleeping, Deja?"

"I'm not, except—" That's as far as I get before Mom does two things: one normal, the other not. She talks over me, like always, but she also gently puts her hand around the back of my neck and pulls my head forward so it's resting on her shoulder.

"You've got to take care of yourself," Mom whispers. "A good mom takes care of herself. That's why I wasn't a good mom to you, Deja. I didn't take care of myself, so how in the world was I gonna take care of a baby, a child, and then a young woman? I'm so sorry."

I've heard Mom say I'm sorry to me or Grams a thousand times, and I've never believed it. Until now. It's not just her tone that seems different. *She* seems different. Calm. Together. Maybe it's having four generations of women in a circle around a table. It doesn't matter that the table is in the workhouse visiting area. It doesn't matter that people in uniforms are looking on. And it doesn't matter that in ten minutes she's headed back to her cell and we're headed home. What matters isn't the past or the future, but right now. This moment with Heaven.

"What you going to do about school?" Mom asks. "You said you'd stay in school."

"It starts on Monday," I remind her. "I'm in the pregnant and parenting program."

"They didn't have such a thing back in the day," Mom says.

"It's going to work out." I'm hoping it's not just wishful thinking, but I'm confident. Like Molly said.

"It's almost time." Grams points at the clock. She hands Heaven back to Mom. Mom kisses her on the forehead. I see Heaven's tiny hands reach up to touch Mom's face.

The end of visiting time always gets loud, lots of crying, lots of laughing, lots of sharing. 'Cept I don't hear anything but the tiny sounds from Heaven.

Grams must sense it too, because she doesn't say a word: let's let Mom have all the baby's attention.

For the last five minutes, we sit in silence, in awe. It's like a week ago, two people were born into this world: Heaven and this version of Mom. As I watch Mom look at Heaven with such love, it makes me think that's how she used to look at me once. And maybe, with what I'm doing for her, that's the way she's gonna look at me again, and then all the time.

The CO tells us it's time to leave, so I stand and break the silence with good-byes. I sling my just-for-visiting baby bag over my shoulder, glad we didn't have to use the spare diapers. Then I reach out my arms for Heaven, but Mom shakes her head like she doesn't want to give her back to me. The CO yells at her and she hands the baby to Grams. Mom stands, takes a step toward the cells, then turns back around. She runs to me and hugs me so tight I can't breathe. It hurts in the best way.

11

TWO WEEKS AFTER THE BIRTH

There she is: Yasmin Franklin, my only enemy. She stands her no-good self right by the door of the nursery, acting like she owns the place. Like always, she's talking on her phone so loud she don't need one. She got her baby strapped to her back like Luke's daughter was a piece of luggage.

"Deja Gibson?" I hear a voice from behind. I turn to see Leigh Davis, a girl I know from middle school. Not an enemy like Yasmin, not a friend like Shanice, just a girl I knew once.

"Hey, Leigh." We slowly push our strollers together.

I introduce her to Heaven, who's sleeping like the dead after keeping me up all night. I tell Leigh about raising Heaven for a few months until Mom gets out of County. She asks a lot of questions, like she's actually interested.

She lifts her baby from the stroller and shows him off like a prize. He's a cute little boy—Tray—probably the second cutest baby on planet Earth. I don't ask about the daddy, 'cos I figure if she wanted to tell me, she would.

"We don't want to be late the first day." I angle the stroller toward the doorway. Yasmin's finally gone in.

"I see you haven't changed, still following all the rules," Leigh says, laughs.

I laugh too. That's a sound I want Heaven to hear a lot.

The nursery is full of teenage girls with babies and a couple with babies in their bellies. I know some of these girls. Others I made a point not to know. I try not to judge 'em for choosing the life. I just avoid them and their troubles.

But now I gotta be here with the rest of them to start the day. The program director,

Mrs. Hartwell, introduces herself, the other teachers, and the staff. Yasmin's texting, paying no attention.

Other girls ask questions, and all the adults take time to answer them, really polite—although a little loud, since they have to talk over crying babies. Once a couple kids start to cry it's like that game of dominos I see old men play at the park. Soon almost the whole room is a tear factory, 'cept Heaven, who's still out cold.

Mrs. Hartwell starts talking about the best ways to help your baby stop crying, and pretty soon everybody's talking at once: it's one big sound storm. I want to hold Heaven, but I don't want to disturb her sleep. That's the hardest part—not me not sleeping, not her not sleeping, but me not holding Heaven in my arms twenty-four-seven. The thought that I'm going have to leave her here and go to a classroom slams me with fear and loss. How is Mom dealing with this?

"So what you doing here?" Yasmin almost hisses at me under the racket.

I don't answer her, don't even look at her. My plan is not to say a word to her: not hello, not good-bye, nothing unless she apologizes for stealing Luke away from me. But she won't 'cos sorry ain't a four letter word and that's about the only kind of words she knows.

"You all stuck up or something?" she asks. "Seems we in the same boat."

I put my hands on the stroller so she won't see 'em shaking.

"Guess Luke dropped you just in time." I can hear the smirk in her voice now. "If he'd stayed with you he coulda been stuck with that ugly-ass little—"

"Yasmin, shut your mouth!" I snap. She can say what she wants about me, but I won't let her talk that way about Heaven.

Everybody turns toward us.

"You gonna make me?" she yells like an angry six-year-old.

"No."

"What I thought." Her baby's crying, but she pays no attention. "You a coward."

"Grow up," I say. Because one thing's clear to me. Yasmin's a mother, but she's no adult. She's a kid with a kid. I'm better than that. I have to be.

12

THREE WEEKS AFTER THE BIRTH

"So how's it going, Deja?" asks Miss Chandler, the chipper school counselor.

"It's harder than I thought." Understatement of the year. It's like I got a checklist that never has anything checked off: feeding, changing diapers, bathing, dressing and undressing, over and over again.

With school started, Malik and Shanice aren't around as much. They'll text to say "What's up?" and "How's it going?" but I know they're too busy to hear the full answers. And Grams just seems tired all the time. Her arms start to ache after just a few minutes of holding Heaven.

Whenever she has to make another milk-and-diaper run, on top of her usual trips to the store, she comes back shuffling like a zombie. Mom's still happy to see us visit, but she's stopped calling, saying it's too expensive. It's all on me.

"How do these other girls do it?" I ask. "I mean, I only have to do this for a few months, then I can get on with my life, but the rest of them, it's forever."

"Everybody's different, Deja." Miss Chandler keeps talking, telling me lots of things I already know. Sometimes I feel like I know more than all these white grown-ups combined.

"Deja, are you listening?"

"I'm sorry, I'm just really tired," I admit. "I'm gonna ask Mrs. Hartwell to build a nap time in the schedule just like we used to have in kindergarten. We all could use the sleep. I'd say that's the biggest problem."

Miss Chandler laughs. I look around her desk for pictures of kids—she's got none. She can't know.

"Well, we do have another alternative. HISD offers an online school."

"I don't have a computer at home."

Miss Chandler starts listing programs that might be able to help get me both a computer and high-speed Internet access. She's a lot like Mom about programs.

"I don't know," I say. "I like school."

"When you show up." I've been waiting for that. School's been in session for ten days and I've missed three, been late twice. I use Heaven as the excuse, but she's not the only reason.

"What can we do to get you here more consistently?" she asks, ready to answer with another program.

"Kick Yasmin Franklin out of school."

"Yes, I understand there's some friction there." I stop myself from snapping back that there's no way she *understands*.

Heaven's a place with no mistakes, and Hell's where you go when you've made a ton of them. But seeing Yasmin with Luke's baby every day puts me in that place in between. It reminds me of what my life could have been. I could've been the one with Luke's baby. And the worst of it is I don't know if that would've been a mistake.

Maybe you can never really know.

"Are there any girls in the program you get along with?" she asks.

I talk a little about Leigh, and Miss Chandler seems all pleased, like she won some prize.

"I know it's hard, Deja, and some days will be harder than others, but just know that everybody is pulling for you, and we're here to help however we can. You know that, right?"

I nod, because that's what she expects. No point mentioning that everyone who's ever promised to help me has let me down.

13

FOUR WEEKS AFTER THE BIRTH

Heaven won't stop crying.

I've tried everything: rock, rattle, book, backrub, tickle, cuddle, but nothing works. It's bad enough at home or school, but it's worst when there are other people around, stressed out strangers like everyone standing in line for visiting hours at the workhouse.

Unlike the weekend visits, which are more relaxed, everybody's tense and tired for the night visits. Kids have been in school, parents have been at work, and grandparents like Grams are just tired. I never really noticed how tired

Grams always is. Maybe it's gotten worse lately. It's like every day that Heaven's with us, Grams grows a month older.

The guard calls us, one of the female ones. She ignores Heaven, like paying attention to the cutest baby in the world would make her seem not so tough. All she says is, "Good luck, girlie, your mom is in a rage."

Mom's sitting way at the back of the room, and she ain't smiling. As soon as we get to her table, she puts her arms out like I'm supposed to drop Heaven into them, like she don't even have to ask to hold her or ask how we're doing. "She's been crying a lot," I tell her, even though that's obvious.

When she hears that, Mom gives me a *told you so* smirk. Why does she seem happy to see her daughter— make that *daughters*—miserable?

I shoot a look at Grams. What's going on here? What happened? Where's the happy, calm mother we saw the last time we were here?

"She senses you're tense, that's why she's crying," Mom says. "That's what Erin said."

"I wish I could've met her," I say loud enough

to be heard over baby cries.

Mom starts rocking Heaven a little too hard, too fast. "Erin left me."

So that's it. Mom's mad that Erin's gone and she's taking it out on us. Carla Gibson never forgives people when they disappear from her life. Even though she does that to us all the time and expects us to be fine with it.

Grams sighs. "You knew the doula program would end, Carla."

"Isn't Erin doing the parenting group?" I ask.

"She is," says Mom coldly. "I'm not."

"Why not?" Grams asks.

Mom's eyes flash. "I don't answer to you. I'm not twelve years old anymore."

Grams makes the snorting sound. "You didn't listen to me when you were twelve and that's why you're in here." Grams's voice booms, but the noisiest human in the room is still Heaven. How could something so tiny be so loud?

"You know what, Coretta, I never heard you say no." When Mom gets mad at Grams she calls her by her first name as an act of disrespect.

"When I'd be riding high, bringing home handfuls of bills, I never heard you turn down the steaks I bought, the gift I gave you. You want the good, but you don't want to put up with the bad. And that's me, Coretta, that's me."

Now they're at it, and Heaven's in the middle of the same argument those two have been having all my life, trying to answer one question: *who is to blame?*

"Come on, Deja, get the baby, we're leaving," Grams says.

I stand and hold my arms out, but Mom's not moving a muscle. "Mom, can I have Heaven?"

"It's a stupid name," Mom says as she hands Heaven back to me. "It sounds like something Aunt Beatrice put you up to. If she's Heaven, does that make me Hell? Is that what you're all trying to say? That because you're on the outs, you're better than me? Is that it?"

She's talking loud enough to get everyone's attention, visitor and guard alike. "Would you please keep it down," some middle-aged woman snaps at us.

"What did you say?" Now Mom's got

somebody else to turn her fury on.

Two of the COs—one male, one female—come over and get in Mom's face. The guy's got his hand on his baton. The lady tries to talk to Mom in a low voice, but whatever she says just gets Mom more worked up.

"You all think you're better than me, is that it?" she shrieks. "You ain't nothing, not one of you. Not you, Mom, not you, Deja, and not that crying sack of crap Heaven. I should've never—"

"Shut up, Mom!" I shout. Heaven cries so loud I'm afraid that she'll never stop.

14

"I told you, Deja, I'm done." Grams won't even look up from the pile of laundry she's sorting. "I'm not going back there again just so Carla can throw everything I've ever tried to do for her back in my face."

"But I can't go if you don't go." Grams is my legal guardian, and since I'm under eighteen I can't visit without her. "That means Mom won't get to see Heaven."

"She should'a thought that through before she went and threw a tantrum, shouldn't she?" snaps Grams.

"Please, Grams," I beg. "She didn't mean it.

She loves Heaven, you know that. She'll want to see her."

I don't say what else I'm thinking: that the longer Mom goes without seeing Heaven, the more that love for her baby—our baby—will twist into anger at us, at herself, at the world. When you're looking at Heaven, all you see is a beautiful little life. Even when she's crying, even when she's smelling like her diaper's full of rotting eggs. But when you're not looking at Heaven, when she's not right in front of you, what you remember is the crying and the smelliness, and you wonder what's the point—you wonder why you care.

I don't want Mom to start thinking that way. I want her to see Heaven in person as often as she can, to remember that Heaven's worth caring about, worth turning her life around for.

Grams makes me beg her before she finally agrees to go. "But I'm not taking that godawful bus again," she says. So now it's up to me to find another way to get us to County.

When I call Molly and ask her for a ride, she agrees, but I can tell she doesn't like it. Just like

I can tell she hasn't really liked her last few visits since they've been about Heaven, not about her and me and library books.

So we get to County, wait in line, go through the screening, and there's no Mom.

"She's in sep," a guard says. That's County lingo for separation.

I ask why and they won't say. Whatever the answer, it's never good: either punishment for breaking the rules, or protection from hurting herself or others. Like us.

A whole night wasted, and Mom's letting me down again.

***

Next day, I'm so tired it hurts. Seems like whenever I have a second to catch my breath, I end up fighting tears. Every time there's a break between classes, I have to run to the bathroom. Take big gulps of air, cry a little, splash my face, don't bother with makeup 'cos I gotta run to my next class. My hair's a mess. I barely got time to make Heaven look decent—I don't have any time for myself. Not even a minute. I miss

Malik, Shanice, regular school, regular life.

At the end of the day Leigh and I leave the building together, pushing our strollers side by side. Yasmin's standing in front of us out on the sidewalk, waiting for a ride I guess. She's on her phone, texting. Luke's daughter might as well not exist. Yasmin doesn't miss her old life because she's still living it.

"What's up with you?" Leigh asks me. "You been out of it all day."

I start to tell her everything, thinking at least she'll understand, but she don't seem interested.

"Stop whining, Deja," Leigh snaps. "I mean, for you, this is something you got to do for a few more weeks until your mom gets home. You got it easy compared to us."

"Ain't nothing about this easy."

"Like I don't know that." She's a year younger than me but somehow acts like she knows more.

"What's with the attitude, Leigh?"

"I'd ask you the same, Deja," Leigh says. "You act all like you got all the answers, like you're not one of us, like you're better than us 'cos you didn't get pregnant like we did."

I got no answer to that. No answer that don't prove her right and make me feel ashamed. Finally I say, "I don't think I'm better than you. I just think we're different. We got different situations. I'm here 'cos of my mom's choices, you're here 'cos of your own."

She shakes her head. "That's exactly what I'm talking about. Look, nobody's life turns out perfect. Some of my life is the choices I made, some of it's the choices other people made, some of it ain't got nothin' to do with choice at all. I'm doing the best I can with what I got. You can judge me all you want, you can think I deserve to be here and you don't, but keep your mouth shut about it, because we all got bigger things to worry about than your pride."

I look away so Leigh won't see the tears fill my eyes. Seems Heaven ain't the only one who cries easy these days. But it's like Leigh's holding up a mirror, and the reflection's showing someone childish, selfish—someone like Mom.

A few feet away from us, Yasmin's still texting. She must sense I'm watching her, because now she looks up and gives me a death glare.

"Yeah, that's right," she calls to me. "I'm texting him. Telling him how he's lucky I'm the one who had his baby, 'cos Gibson babies turn out ugly and stupid . . ."

I'm lunging at her almost before she gets the words out. She's ready for me, blocks my slap with one hand and goes for my face with the other, all the while yelling things I'm glad I'm too angry to hear. Leigh's yelling too, but I ain't hearing her either, and I'm glad of that too.

Yasmin shoves me backward, and now I'm stumbling, and now I'm slamming into something solid—solid but not strong, 'cos it's tipping backward—

And I hear Heaven crying.

It's all happening in slow motion. The stroller tipping, me falling, trying to turn, trying to catch myself, trying to catch Heaven before the stroller hits the ground and she spills out onto the hard pavement . . .

Then time freezes. Leigh's standing next to me, holding Heaven's stroller with one hand and grabbing my arm with the other. I stagger a little as I get my balance back and Leigh carefully sets the stroller upright. Heaven's still in here, still strapped in. But she's crying louder than an ambulance siren.

I'm on my knees, checking her over, making sure she really isn't hurt. No scrapes, no dirt on her clothes. The stroller didn't fall all the way over—she never touched the ground. But all the things that could've happened are running through my mind—Heaven with a bloody face, a cracked head.

Leigh keeps saying, "She's OK, Deja," and I keep sobbing, "I'm so sorry, Heaven, I'm so sorry." Heaven's just crying, not knowing what's going on. Not knowing that her stupid sister made a mistake that could've hurt her—could've even messed up her life forever.

Off to the side, Yasmin says something foul, goes back to her own stroller, and wheels it away. I can barely remember why I was so angry with her a few seconds ago. Looking down at Heaven, thinking about what could've happened, I feel like I'm no better than Yasmin.

No better than my mom.

15

"Deja, you awake?"

I try to lift my head off the kitchen table, but it feels heavier than usual. There's drool on the textbook, which was beat-up enough as it was.

"Just tired," I mumble to Grams, who's sitting across from me peeling potatoes.

"Heaven's crying," Grams says. "Probably needs a diaper change."

And now I hear it, coming from the other room. Just the thought of standing makes my legs ache. "Grams, could you do it this time? Could you go check . . ."

"I got dinner to make."

69

"Well, I got homework!"

"You took this on, Deja," Grams says. "It was your decision."

"I know." I force myself to sit up straight in the chair. Weighed down by all the reasons I did this, all the things I thought would change because of it. I'd have this little girl who loved me because she thought I was her mother, and I'd have a mother who loved me more than she had in a long time because I did something so hard for her. But I know now that none of that's happening. Heaven just sees me as a face and a set of arms. Mom just sees me as an extended babysitting service, 'cept I ain't even getting paid. "I know, Grams."

"Deja, if you can't handle this, then we need to talk about other options."

I don't have to ask what kind of options she means. Dewayne, Joseph, Rae—all my half-sibs went the "other options" route. The thought of putting Heaven into foster care—even temporarily—is enough to send me over the edge.

"Could you just back off?" I snap. "Could everyone just *back off*!"

Ever since what happened at school last week, I've been walking on eggshells. Avoiding Yasmin, ignoring her put-downs, that's been the easy part. The hard part is looking at Heaven, looking at myself, and believing that this'll still turn out all right. That I can still give my sister everything I promised her.

Heaven starts crying louder now, like she knows I need a reason to leave. I get up.

"Don't you walk out on me," says Grams. "We're not done talking."

"Yeah, Grams, we are done." I fling the words over my shoulder and head into my room.

Don't you walk out on me. Why shouldn't I? It runs in the family.

My memory jumps to a hot day like this one—Mom and Grams screaming at each other.

I was eight. Mom had just finished two years at Gatesville, which was hours away, so we'd rarely gone to visit. She'd been home maybe a week before she started running with her old crew. For as much I saw her, she could've just stayed in Gatesville. Only this was worse. Her not seeing me at Gatesville was about distance.

At home, it was about her decisions. So Grams and Mom were screaming at each other, and Mom said she was leaving. Grams didn't try to stop her from going, but she wouldn't let her take me. "I got legal custody, you got nothing!" Grams screamed.

"I'm her mother! I love her!" Mom screamed back. Even at eight, I didn't believe her.

So Mom packed her few things and started out the door. Then she set down her bag, hugged me, kissed me, and broke my heart again.

I think I said, "Don't go, Mommy," or something like that. So many scenes like this, they get blurred sometimes.

"Nobody wants me here," Mom had said, breaking the hug. She and Grams started again so loud, they didn't hear my crying in the corner, when I said, "I do, Mom."

Grams said, "When you get settled you make sure you get me your address."

"I don't want you visiting and I don't want you writing. You don't need no address."

All the anger seemed to leave Grams's body as Mom left the door with these words trailing behind her: "I need an address so I can tell them where to find your overdosed dead body."

I rock Heaven in my arms and remind myself that Mom's still alive. She still has a chance to make the right choices.

She didn't do it for me. Maybe she'll do it for Heaven.

16

Usually Sundays are the best part of the week—everybody over at our house, talking and sharing good food. But lately Sundays are more exhausting than school days. I can't wait for everyone to leave.

The big dinner's over now, and only Aunt Beatrice, Shanice, and Malik are still here. Shanice and Malik stare at their phones like they're thinking *when do I get out of here?* But they can't leave till Aunt Beatrice does. She's in the kitchen with Grams, helping with dishes. I've taken Heaven into the bathroom to give her a bath. I'm just lifting her out of the little plastic tub and toweling her off when someone knocks on the bathroom door.

"Deja, I need to get in there before we leave." Aunt Beatrice.

"Be out in just a minute."

"Couldn't you have waited to give the baby her bath until after we were gone?" she huffs.

"It's almost her bedtime," I call through the door as I put her fresh diaper on. "I had to get her washed up before then."

Aunt Beatrice mumbles something else that I'm glad I can't hear. I finish getting Heaven back into her clothes, balance her on my hip, and open the bathroom door to switch places with Aunt Beatrice. "All yours."

"It's a mess in here," she says, stepping into the bathroom.

"I'll finish cleaning up when you've done your business," I retort. "Unless you wanna help for once?"

"Don't sass me!" Beatrice rounds on me.

"Well, don't get on me for not cleaning up

when you acted like you was about to break down the door. I give Heaven a bath three times a week and I always clean up after, and I don't see nobody offering to give me a hand."

Now Grams is next to me. "Deja, let it go."

"And how am I supposed to do that?" I shouldn't be shouting so close to Heaven's sensitive ears, but I can't help it. "You said you were going to help me. You promised. But you're just like her."

"Just like who?" says Grams.

"My mom. You get mad at her for breaking her promises, then you do the same. You all said you'd support me, but I'm not seeing it."

Malik and Shanice have looked up from their phones. Shanice has tears in her eyes.

Malik says, "Deja, we want to help. We just don't know how. You don't text us back when we ask how you're doin'. You never ask us to come over or to do anything. We never know if you want us around or if we'll just be in the way . . ."

"You acted like you was ready to do this all on your own," adds Shanice. "You had all these plans for how to take care of the baby, for how to handle everything. We don't know where we fit into that. And you ain't told us."

Now I'm the one fighting tears. Here I've been thinking I'm alone in this. Maybe all I needed to do was reach out. Reach out and trust that somebody'd reach back.

"Come over after school," I say. "Once a week. Help with Heaven's bath. Help me do her laundry. Help me read to her. Or even better, bring over some books from the library—I got no time to go myself. And diapers—we run outa diapers in like two hours, and . . ."

My voice is getting all chokey, and I feel like a fool standing here crying and talking about diapers. Heaven makes a happy burbling sound like this is all part of her master plan.

I turn to Grams. "And you, Grams—I know you got a lot to deal with already. I know you ain't got the energy for a baby. But just once in a while, just one or two little things—watch her for just a few minutes, feed her just one night a week. It'd make a difference, Grams."

Grams reaches out, puts her hand on my shoulder, and squeezes it like she's wringing all the moisture out of a sponge. She says nothing, which says everything.

17

Mom's made a rare call, short and cheap, to say she's out of sep and she needs us to come to the next visiting hours. Needs, not wants.

The waiting seems to take longer when it's for something you need. Mom's at the back table again—not a good sign. But when she sees us, I swear her smile lights up the ugly, dim room. Hugs, kisses, all around. Then we sit down. I ask Mom if she wants to hold Heaven.

"More than anything in the world." There's something about Mom's tone: she means it.

I hand Heaven over and set my baby bag on the table. Mom's all into Heaven, so me and

Grams just sit silent, listening to conversations around us. They're all the same, it seems: people talking about getting out, getting on with their lives, turning over a new leaf. Every single one of them, Mom included, believes it, so all of us on the outs have to believe them too, no matter how many times we've been burned. Each time they go in, they say it's the last time. We believe even if we know better. We believe because if we don't believe, then how can Mom believe in herself?

Mom hands Heaven over to Grams and starts asking me about school. I tell her how bad it is and she's all full of PC. That's the good thing about County time, it's contact visit time.

Then Mom says, "I got something to tell you both." And every other conversation in the building—at least in my head—stops dead. There's just silence.

But Mom doesn't say anything, like she's afraid or something.

"What is it, Carla?" Grams asks. She's fearing the worst, I can tell.

"I can get into a program," Mom says. "It's supposed to be one of the best—well, one of the best for people like me. But I need to go right after release. It's twenty-eight days."

My heart sinks and even the happy baby sounds Heaven's making can't raise it.

"Take the baby for a minute, Carla," Grams says. Then she rises and motions for me to join her. We walk toward the corner of the gray room, not saying a word until our backs are against the wall.

"Can you do it, Deja?" Grams ask, really soft.

I take a deep breath. "No," I say. "Not alone."

Grams nods. "I'm just so tired," she says. "But it's only another month."

"We've got Malik and Shanice too," I remind her. "And I'm going to talk to the school counselor about doing the online classes."

Seems like there's nothing else to say. We don't really have a decision here—Mom's made it for us. But for once in her life, it's obvious it's the right one. She's going right to rehab, not back home with all its temptations. Like every time before, she's making promises. But this time, I trust she's gonna keep 'em, 'cos she's got me, Grams, and now Heaven.

We turn to walk back toward Mom. There she is, cradling Heaven in her right arm. Her left arm she's got one of the board books I had in my bag. She looks ten years younger. I almost want to run to the table.

Leigh's right. I don't have all the answers. But there are some things that I'm learning, slowly, to understand. Like hope. Like Heaven.

AFTERWORD

As of 2014, it's estimated that more than 2.7 million children in the United States have a parent behind bars. About one in five of those kids are teenagers. While having parents in prison presents challenges at any age, it may be particularly hard for teenagers, as they try to find their way in the world.

The *Locked Out* series explores the realities of parental incarceration through the eyes of teens dealing with it. These stories are fictional, but the experiences that Patrick Jones writes about are daily life for many youths.

The characters deal with racism, stigma,

shame, sadness, confusion, and isolation—common struggles for children with parents in prison. Many teens are forced to move from their homes, schools, or communities as their families cope with their parents' incarcerations.

These extra challenges can affect teens with incarcerated parents in different ways. Kids often struggle in school—they are at increased risk for skipping school, feeling disconnected from classmates, and failing classes. They act out and test boundaries. And they're prone to taking risks, like using substances or engaging in other illegal activities.

In addition, studies have shown that youth who are involved in the juvenile justice system are far more likely than their peers to have a parent in the criminal justice system. In Minnesota, for example, boys in juvenile correctional facilities are ten times more likely than boys in public schools to have a parent currently incarcerated. This cycle of incarceration is likely caused by many factors. These include systemic differences in the distribution of wealth and resources, as well as bias within policies and practices.

The *Locked Out* series offers a glimpse into this complex world. While the books don't sugarcoat reality, each story offers a window of hope. The teen characters have a chance to thrive despite difficult circumstances. These books highlight the positive forces that make a difference in teens' lives: a loving, consistent caregiver; other supportive, trustworthy adults; meaningful connections at school; and participation in sports or other community programs. Indeed, these are the factors in teens' lives that mentoring programs around the country aim to strengthen, along with federal initiatives such as My Brother's Keeper, launched by President Obama.

This series serves as a reminder that just because a parent is locked up, it doesn't mean kids need to be locked out.

—Dr. Rebecca Shlafer
Department of Pediatrics,
University of Minnesota

AUTHOR ACKNOWLEDGMENTS

Thanks to Dan Marcou, Rae Baker, and Chloe Britzius for reading and commenting on this manuscript. Also thanks to Erica Gerrity and Debby Prudhomme for their support on this book.

ABOUT THE AUTHOR

Patrick Jones is the author of more than twenty-five novels for teens. He has also written two nonfiction books about combat sports: *The Main Event*, on professional wrestling, and *Ultimate Fighting*, on mixed martial arts. He has spoken to students at more than one hundred alternative schools and has worked with incarcerated teens and adults for more than a decade. Find him on the web at www.connectingya.com and on Twitter: @PatrickJonesYA.

RETURNING TO NORMAL

PATRICK JONES

TAKING SIDES

PATRICK JONES

GUARDING SECRETS

PATRICK JONES

RAISING HEAVEN

PATRICK JONES

DOING RIGHT

PATRICK JONES

CHECK OUT ALL OF THE TITLES IN THE LOCKED OUT SERIES

THE ALTERNATIVE

FAILING CLASSES.

DROPPING OUT.

JAIL TIME.

When it seems like there are no other options left, Rondo Alternative High School might just be the last chance a student needs.